FRIENDS FOREVER

John M. Solov

To order additional copies of this book, contact:
Xlibris
844-714-8691
www.Xlibris.com
Orders@Xlibris.com

ISBN: Softcover   978-1-6641-0990-2
       EBook   978-1-6641-0989-6

Print information available on the last page.

Rev. date: 01/22/2022

DEDICATION

I would like to dedicate this book to all the children and adults in the World who are willing to really try and accept people with different cultures, beliefs, skin colors, and are willing to work together to become real friends to make this planet a better place in which to live and grow. My children are so much a part of me. I would like to thank them for helping me to view the world through their eyes and to grow up along with them.

This story came about from my daughter's first sleepover at our home.

It was late on a Saturday night and my daughter, Heather was upstairs in her bedroom talking away with her girlfriend. My wife informed me that I needed to go upstairs and tell the girls they have to go to sleep or that they would have to be separated. I walked up the stairs and Heather's door was almost closed, slightly ajar. Neither one of the girls heard me. They were in the middle of a conversation. Meghan said to Heather before she goes to sleep she is going to pray to her lord, her Savior or something to that effect. She also said that she is going to pray for others. Heather said, "It is good to pray for others." Heather also stated that she is Jewish and that she has been taught that the Savior is going to come. I am not a depressive individual, yet tears welled up in my eyes. Here are two children of different faiths and different opinions, different religious educations. Both are still innocent. How lucky they were, I thought, able to talk of things grownups often have great difficulty speaking of without anger and prejudice. I was humbled by these two little girls. It took what seemed to be a few moments to regain my composure before I knocked on the door and walked in. "All right ladies!" I said. "It is time for the two of you to go to sleep." I don't know if it was cowardice of me or not to pass the buck or just plain self-preservation. I blamed the reprimand on my wife. "Heather, your mother told me to tell you, "You have Sunday school in the morning and Meghan you've got Church. We're going to have to separate you two if you do not go to sleep really soon." Heather looked up at me with those big blue eyes of hers, (like I had just condemned her to a life of solitude) and said, "Daddy we are not tired. Would you please read us a story before we go to sleep?" How could a Daddy resist? "Well alright," I said. "But then it is lights out!" Heather looked at Meghan with an 'I got the best of him' smile and proceeded to get off her book shelf a novel that would have carried me into the next day to read. "Oh no, young ladies! If you want me to read that I will only read a chapter. Or you can pick from these two stories." I took two very short paged books from the shelf, which they both agreed would be ok. Then it would be lights out. I sat on the end of the trundle bed and read the stories. When they were over I went to turn the reading light out and Heather said, "Daddy we're still not tired." At this time, I got a little upset and said, "Ok now, it's not your Mommy talking, it's me! I'm going to separate you!" "No Daddy, wait!" Heather reverted back to her toddler days. "Daaady, can't you make us up a story like you used to do for Louis and me when I was weel lidddle?" "Heather, I am so rusty; I don't think so. Besides, you can't remember the stories – you were too young." "Yes I do daddy." Heather used her best negotiating skills, what a lawyer she would make! "Ok Heather, if you can name me the story (which was ongoing for several weeks and was never written down, all in my head) I'll make you up a story. Even if it lasts two minutes light are out. As a matter of fact, it will be lights out anyway since I don't have to read. Agreed?" "Yes daddy." "Agreed, Meghan?" "Yes Mr. Solov." "There are no toes crossed or fingers crossed or any tricks like that, understand?" Both of them said, "Yes." I knew that there was no way Heather could remember the name of the story. Sleep it is, or so I thought. "Daddy it was the Goobley, Gobbley, Goobley, Goobley Monster stories. They came from the Planet of Goobley." I couldn't believe it! Just shows how much they absorb at young ages. "Daddy they looked awful, smelled bad, yet had great knowledge, and extremely kind hearts." At first Heather explained we were very cautious and still were as time went by. It is always good to be cautious. As time went by we learned a lot from each other. When they went back to their planet they had a better understanding of us too.

"Ok Heather and Meghan. As agreed I will tell you the story." I turned the lights out and sat at the foot of the bed. "Meghan since you are our guest will you give us the honor of picking out the topic (what you want me to make up the story about). "Mr. Solov, could you make up a story about a Princess?" "I'll try, I said." I looked at Heather and said, "You are my little Princess," and looked at Meghan and said, "You are my visiting Princess."

The words seemed to flow out of my mouth. When I was done the two Princesses fell right to sleep holding each other's hand. They looked like sleeping Angels. I wanted to take pictures of them, however, I didn't want to take a chance of waking them up. Down I went to the computer room and typed to the best of my recollection of what was said. Before I knew it, the sun had come up and I'd had no sleep.

Several weeks later, by chance, I met an artist at my son's soccer game. We started talking. She became the artist for the book. Thank you Mini-Kong for your hard work. Thank you for reading on. May you be blessed always.

Prologue

I want to thank all the parents, grandparents, children, and educators who have read this short story with long story messages. For all people who have hope and faith that one day we can set aside our differences that cause prejudice and hatred among us, this book is meant to help bridge that gap. This book is for people to help realize that there really are no boundaries when it comes to health, education, and human rights. The truth of the matter is, if we do not give these qualities a chance to work, our world as we know it will be doomed to suffering and hardships unimaginable in our modern day societies.

We are blessed with choices, both easy and hard. May our choices be the right ones. Only time will tell!

Once upon a time many years ago there were two princesses who lived far far away from each other. They lived a whole ocean apart yet they knew each other by hearing stories of each other from sailors and merchants who would trade spices, clothing, and other items needed or desired and bring them to faraway places. One of the princess's names was Meghan and the other princess's name was Heather. They were two of the best liked and respected princesses ever to be found.

Unlike some of the people in high places, they were very nice. They had wonderful manners and were thoughtful of other people. They never put anyone down for not having as much as they did. They would never tease someone or make fun of them. They would even share their toys with people whom other princesses would not. Heather and Meghan wanted so badly to meet each other in person.

One-day, Heather wrote a wonderful note to Meghan: "Dear Meghan, I would love to meet you in person. It is as if I know you already. However, you are so far away! Goodness knows no distance. A friendship to be made has no barriers. I am going to place this note in a bottle and pray that it gets to you in a reasonable length of time. If I give the note to one of the sailors or merchants, it may take years or maybe never arrive to you. So I will pray that the currents will carry my message straight to you."

With those thoughts in mind Heather walked down to the beach and placed the bottle with the note in it in the next wave.

Like a powerful hand the bottle was swept up and carried away in the wave's palm. The moon shone high in the heaven above and the beautiful stars twinkled and winked at Princess Heather, as if confirming her message and prayer that it would make the trip safe and sound to Princess Meghan.

A day turned into two. Two into three. Three into four. Four into five. Five into six. Six into seven. One week into two. Two weeks into three. Three into four.

As if by magic Princess Meghan knew that a message was awaiting for her at the beach.

Even though she was the princess of the land she asked her mother the Queen if it was OK to go to the beach for a moment and listen to the sounds of the waves making music on the sands as they land.

Her mother said that it was OK. The full moon was high in the sky and she knew that there would be enough light for her daughter the Princess.

So Princess Meghan went down to the beach and there in the sand was a bottle that glowed under the moonlight like a million diamonds or the stars above.

She dusted the bottle off and noticed a note in the bottle. Excitedly the princess took the bottle into the castle and up to her room. There she read the note. Princess Meghan was a good reader even though she was only six years old. See, she practiced reading a lot. She could not wait until the next day to write her note back to Princess Heather.

Princess Meghan sat down and wrote the following: "Dear Princess Heather, your note did arrive safe and sound. I would love to meet you too! Please come if you can and spend some time with me. A smart Princess always has her doors open to someone who has wonderful manners, is kind, and good of heart. I will ask my parents if it is ok. (And it was, they said "yes") Please find a way to come and meet me. Your friend Princess Meghan. I will place this note in the bottle and take it back to the ocean in the morning."

Meghan placed the note into the ocean as she said and again the ocean's hand lifted the bottle and swept it away.

One day turned into two, two turned into three, three into four, four into five, five into six, six into seven. One week into two, two weeks into three, three into four weeks.

The moon shone brightly as one big, bright circle in the sky. The stars twinkled and winked in their magical rhythm to the waves' symphony.

By special delivery, a bottle was delivered to the feet of Princess Heather. She bent down, picked it up, and brushed the sand off the bottle. Excitedly Princess Heather brought the bottle to her room and read the note.

Princess Heather was a great reader too for she always read anything that she could get her hands on and always paid close attention in school. The note was from her friend Princess Meghan who lived across the great ocean. Princess Heather asked her father the King and her mother the Queen if she could take the journey to see her friend, Princess Meghan. "Yes," her parents replied, for true friendships have no distance too far nor barrier too great.

They found the means to build a huge ship with bright pink sails, Princess Heather's favorite color. Off it went with the currents, the same currents that led the bottle to Princess Meghan in the first place.

When the ship arrived, Princess Meghan was already waiting at the beach and hugged her friend, Princess Heather. She brought her to her castle to meet her parents, the King and Queen.

Soon after a wonderful dinner

The two princesses went to bed and fell fast asleep, dreaming beautiful dreams and awaiting a new day that a new friendship brings.

Printed in the United States
by Baker & Taylor Publisher Services